Rajat
at Aldeburgh
10-11-'90

Rented Rooms

Rented Rooms

Edited
by
David Dabydeen

Dangaroo  Press

Acknowledgements

We wish to thank West Midland Arts for its support towards the publication of this book.

We also with to thank Victor France for his permission to use his photograph for the cover and Fremantle Arts Centre Press who recently published Victor France's photographs and Alan Alexander's poems in a volume entitled *Northline*.

This book is copyright. Apart from any fair dealing for the purposes of private study, research, criticism or review, as permitted under the Copyright Act, no part may be reproduced by any process without written permission. Inquiries should be addressed to the publisher.

Cover: Photograph by Victor France

© David Dabydeen

Dangaroo Press
Australia: P.O. Box 1209, Sydney, New South Wales 2001
Denmark: Pinds Hus, Geding Søvej 21, 8381 Mundelstrup
UK: P.O. Box 186, Coventry CV4 7HG

ISBN 1-871049-40-7

Contents

Preface

Alison Brackenbury:

Yesterday Vivaldi visited me	9
Constellations	10
Rented Rooms	12
Leaving Present	13
Woken	14
Bookkeeping	15

David Dabydeen:

Coolie Odyssey	16
Ma Talking Words	21

Clive Bush:

We Have been speaking all along	23
song for H.	29

Linton Kwesi Johnson:

Sonny's Lettah	31
Reggae fi Dada	34

Rolf Lass:

Life	38
The Wards in Jarndyce	39
Folly	40
Madness	42
Lizzie's Well	43
A Tale of Hoffmann	44

Pauline Melville:

Mixed	45
Hideous Love	45

Homeland	47
Cove and John	48
Stonebridge Park Estate	50
Manadela	51

Notes on Poets 52

Preface

Poems are sometimes selected for anthologies on the basis of unity in geography, gender, race, nationality, chronology, language, style, subject matter or some other shared set of features. *Rented Rooms* came about purely by the logic of binding accidents. Pauline Melville and David Dabydeen were stranded for twenty two hours at Timehri airport, Guyana, waiting for their return plane to London, without water, food, cigarettes, money or reading matter. Guyana at the time was suffering from a shortage of *everything*. Melville had a typescript of poems on her which she passed to Dabydeen to kill time. A few months later Alison Brackenbury was in Birmingham reading at a Poetry Festival at which David Hart, the Literature Director of West Midlands Arts was present. Linton Kwesi Johnson in the meantime had done a reading at the University of Warwick where he had recently been made an Associate Fellow. Both Rolf Lass and Clive Bush teach at the University, and Pauline Melville later registered to do a postgraduate thesis there. David Hart was a frequent visitor to the University's seminar programmes. And so the book came about, the money for its publication generously provided in part by the West Midlands Arts Association.

Alison Brackenbury

Yesterday Vivaldi visited me; and sold me some very expensive concertos

He had only one tune.
And that
a thin finger on pulses:
of spring and the frost,
                           the quick turn of girls' eyes
a tune
to hold against darkness,
to fret
for trumpet, for lute
for flutes; violins
to silver the shabbiness
of many towns
the fool's bowl, the court coat,
a tune he would give:
without sorrow or freedom
again, again

        there is only one tune.

Sell it dearly to live.

Constellations

But my daughter; I wish you could see my daughter
Stretch woolly hands to an Alsatian,
The blunt pale claws scrabble her coat
Flourish their mud down her prim coat.
She calls to the white cat when she wakes,
Is not afraid.

                      Softly you say-
Glancing to the empty window-
She is ignorant, not brave.

Say that there was not a time
We walked through branches with the beasts,
The stars rose: we were not afraid.

Now in our winter we can see
A child scanned before its birth.
Silver fish on a dull screen
Kicking up, out the black stream,
Where have you gone?

Lolled back, she sleeps
In the icy sun, the moss-green pram,
Still with her arms held stiffly out
The wings of a swan. So Cygnus flies -
They tell me - through the winter heaven;
I cannot find him from my book.

That we must, still, be told, then look,
Forcing old lines round fleeing light,
Is that your way? I tremble, see

Bright Castor, Pollux, held and free;
Lovers, beasts, who once they were
Does not disturb them, constant pair.

Look back, past me. White streams of sky
Wheel over; I stand, trying
To track lost stars this night. She was not
Swimming. She was flying.

Rented rooms

Night stole away my reason to be there -
that routine note which missed the post. I came
out of the throaty mist, the New Year's air,
stared, at the dim house which showed no name,
called to a girl, who rattled past her bike,
blowing her fog-damp scarf, winter's hot cheeks.

The first door I pushed open from their hall
gaped a conservatory, shadowed: full
of spoiled ferns once, sweet geraniums.
Now it held bikes, askew. It breathed back all
the cold of first streets, lingering on stairs -
the outside door blows open - no one cares
to clean: from Christmas, ivy curls in sprays,
dark, in rolls of dirt. Who went away
leaving this television blank above
a rolled-up quilt? Quick: drop the printed note
on the hall's floor.

                    It echoes back again
the deep sea chill of fog, the waves of dust,
my wonder at a room's dimmed lights..
Need, then:
the stairs to silence; not to own, but love.

Leaving present

I wonder: what happened to those flowers?
Before a neighbour knocked upon your door
Did you get them into water? If not, they would have died.
So the flower-woman said, screwing up her eyes
Against the light; repeating; they love water.

They were scabious, cool blue. When I returned
I saw them nod, flushed purple, on the hill.
Great butterflies broke up from them, new peacocks
Flashing black wings. The horse reached out to them
Stretching, for a mouthful, but I stopped him.

Untouchable flowers.
To buy them, or to let them die
Is not our end. They rustle through the hands.
They are alive. And what I saw
Came for, is true: the cloud-warm hill: and there
A litter of blue petal, upon your tidy floor.

Woken

They have cut the tops off the grass.
The prisoners say, the seed
Will return its airy head
And plant the world.

Sometimes the prisoners see
Not awake - turning -
A face which passes for a moon:
A woman burning.

There are no prisoners here.
Some time in the night
There was a hand which found my face,
Careless as you, as light.

Bookkeeping

These are not (you understand) the figures
which send cold judgement into the backbone
which leave us, workless, shrunk at home
staring in a sky grown black with leaves.

These are like the ticking of a clock,
the daily sums, a van's new brakes,
three drums of trichloroethylene on the back
of a thrumming lorry; yet they take
a day to make: thin bars of figures. While
I try to balance them, light scurries round
like a glad squirrel. Radio music stales -
until shut off.

                What's left when it is done,
the green book closed? There is no sea to swim
no mouth to kiss. Even the light is gone.
Bookkeepers drink over-sugared tea
lie in dark rooms; are always hunched and tired.

Where I stretch up the low bulb burns and whirls.
And in it, I see him. The dusky gold wing folds
across his face. The feathers' sharp tips smudge
his margins..

sunk, in his own shadows, deep
in scattered ledgers of our petty sins:
he, the tireless angel:
Unaccountably, he sleeps.

David Dabydeen

Coolie Odyssey
(for Ma, d. 1985)

Now that peasantry is in vogue,
Poetry bubbles from peat bogs,
People strain for the old folk's fatal gobs
Coughed up in grates North or North East
'Tween bouts o'living dialect,
It should be time to hymn your own wreck,
Your house the source of ancient song:
Dry coconut shells cackling in the fireside
Smoking up our children's eyes and lungs,
Plantains spitting oil from a clay pot,
Thick sugary black tea gulped down.

The calves hustle to suck,
Bawling on their rope but are beaten back
Until the cow is milked.
Frantic children call to be fed.
Roopram the Idiot goes to graze his father's goats backdam
Dreaming that the twig he chews so viciously in his mouth
Is not a twig.

In a winter of England's scorn
We huddle together memories, hoard them from
The opulence of our masters.

You were always back home, forever
As canefield and whiplash, unchanging
As the tombstones in the old Dutch plot
Which the boys used for wickets playing ball.

Over here Harilall who regularly dodged his duties at the
    marketstall
To spin bowl for us in the style of Ramadhin
And afterwards took his beatings from you heroically
In the style of England losing
Is now known as the local Paki
Doing slow trade in his Balham cornershop.
Is it because his heart is not in business
But in the tumble of wickets long ago
To the roar of wayward boys?
Or is it because he spends too much time
Being chirpy with his customers, greeting
The tight-wrapped pensioners stalking the snow
With tropical smile, jolly small chat, credit?
They like Harilall, these muted claws of Empire,
They feel privileged by his grinning service,
They hear steelband in his voice
And the freeness of the sea.
The sun beams from his teeth.

Heaped up beside you Old Dabydeen
Who on Albion Estate clean dawn
Washed obsessively by the canal bank,
Spread flowers on the snake-infested water,
Fed the gods the food that Chandra cooked,
Bathed his tongue of the creole
Babbled by low-caste infected coolies.
His Hindi chants terrorized the watertoads
Flopping to the protection of bush.
He called upon Lord Krishna to preserve
The virginity of his daughters
From the Negroes,

Prayed that the white man would honour
The end-of-season bonus to Poonai
The canecutter, his strong, only son:
Chandra's womb being cursed by deities
Like the blasted land
Unconquerable jungle or weed
That dragged the might of years from a man.
Chandra like a deaf-mute moved about the house
To his command,

A fearful bride barely come-of-age
Year upon year swelling with female child.
Guilt clenched her mouth
Smothered the cry of bursting apart:
Wrapped hurriedly in a bundle of midwife's cloth
The burden was removed to her mother's safekeeping.
He stamped and cursed and beat until he turned old
With the labour of chopping tree, minding cow,
    building fence
And the expense of his daughters' dowries.
Dreaming of India
He drank rum
Till he dropped dead
And was buried to the singing of Scottish Presbyterian
    hymns
And a hell-fire sermon from a pop-eyed bawling catechist,
By Poonai, lately baptised, like half the village.

Ever so old,
Dabydeen's wife,
Hobbling her way to fowl-pen,
Cussing low, chewing her cud, and lapsed in dream,
Sprinkling rice from her shrivelled hand.

Ever so old and bountiful,
Past where Dabydeen lazed in his mudgrave,
Idle as usual in the sun,
Who would dip his hand in a bowl of dhall and rice -
Nasty man, squelching and swallowing like a low-caste sow -
The bitch dead now!

The first boat chugged to the muddy port
Of King George's Town. Coolies come to rest
In El Dorado,
Their faces and best saris black with soot.
The men smelt of saltwater mixed with rum.
The odyssey was plank between river and land,
Mere yards but months of plotting
In the packed bowel of a white man's boat
The years of promise, years of expanse.
At first the gleam of the green land and the white folk
    and the Negroes,
The earth streaked with colour like a toucan's beak,
Kiskidees flame across a fortunate sky,
Canefields ripening in the sun
Wait to be gathered in armfuls of gold.

I have come back late and missed the funeral.
You will understand the connections were difficult.
Three airplanes boarded and many changes
Of machines and landscapes like reincarnations
To bring me to this library of graves,
This small clearing of scrubland.
There are no headstones, epitaphs, dates.
The ancestors curl and dry to scrolls of parchment.
They lie like texts
Waiting to be written by the children
For whom they hacked and ploughed and saved
To send to faraway schools.

Is foolishness fill your head.
Me dead.
Dog-bone and dry-well
Got no story to tell.
Just how me born stupid is so me gone.
Still we persist before the grave
Seeking fables.
We plunder for the maps of El Dorado
To make bountiful our minds in an England
Starved of gold.

Albion village sleeps, hacked
Out between bush and spiteful lip of river.
Folk that know bone
Fatten themselves on dreams
For the survival of days.
Mosquitoes sing at a nipple of blood.
A green-eyed moon watches
The rheumatic agony of houses crutched up on stilts
Pecked about by huge beaks of wind,
That bear the scars of ancient storms.
Crappeau clear their throats in hideous serenade,
Candleflies burst into suicidal flame.
In a green night with promise of rain
You die.

We mark your memory in songs
Fleshed in the emptiness of folk,
Poems that scrape bowl and bone
In English basements far from home,
Or confess the lust of beasts
In rare conceits
To congregations of the educated
Sipping wine, attentive between courses -

See the applause fluttering from their white hands
Like so many messy table napkins.

Ma Talking Words

You only fool yourself when you say
The woman shallow as the water
She cleanse she make-up in
And you out of your precious depth.
Fact is the world want she
And all you can do is curse cut throat and despair
Or more crazy still
Write poetry:
That is dream and air!
You can't make pickni from word
Howsoever beautiful or raging:
The world don't know word.

Next time you lay down with she
And the white flesh wrench and bite like ratmouth
And she moaning fill you with pride,
But after you feel suck dry, throw-away like eggshell
   or seed,
Think that all-body here know your heart still flesh
   with good
And this village ground never grow more bright boy before
Who move out from mud and walk England
And we who stay back
Mash-mouth and crack
Still feed in you.

And how she go understand all that burden and fruit
You bear for we?
And how she go crave your soul and seed
Who always eat plenty
From different pot?
Book learning you got,
But history done dead, hard like teeth and bone
And white people don't want heal their own scar or hear their own story
And you can't hug them with bruk hand
Or lash sense in them with overseer stick.

Young and fresh and pretty
She swallow the world and get belly,
Rub lipstick on she mouth and make joke,
Nightlong music shake she foot.
All man a-take from she and go their way
Whilst stupid you want stay
Pan love like diamond from dirt
And dream that the world know word.

we have been speaking all along
(for Irma Wahlin)

break lines to bring sanity
each day a journal
cut into
familiar logs along two walls of a woodhouse
split infinite space
of North Sweden cold

out of nature
an order for burning
billets descend from actual corners
crush notes over steady variance of earth spin
random and ordered
left and right disappear
a chair in a wooden room
arrests us
fragile
a broken match in too much perspective

between forest and hearth
the corners are cold
terror by fireside
no stories without shadows
no shadows without fire
tales of earth
dying into proverbs of peace disasters in permanent night

a glazed left window
a right slicing into an infinity landscape
a gaze held steady before snow
colours setting limits to nothing

density of wood chips
concentrate dark light
'towards a corner, a partial matter'

fringe rooms set centres
we must get out of here
there could be a family
or a murder
complaints have already been received
of foreigners performing unnatural acts in our woodshed

I look thru your head at the room you show me
voice of the dead flies from tree to tree til burned
fir tree maiden voiceless
dream rood chopped
birds of a feather on set
tiled bathrooms for repeating
'blood is thicker than water'

carnival relief a last resort
melodrama ressurections
santify private disgust in the public square
    nose a ram's head on a Goya banner
    bodies dismembered impaled on trees
    mouth a grinning moon with teeth
    head horn male celebrants under doll madonna in craced
        rock
    cut flowers erect mother permanently
    all murder unspeakable
    live men laid out
    dead men convulse
    a professional army
    to sweep streets clean

of the poor and young and male
heroes masturbating in aluminium cruisers
under women photographed for a price
caressing their own nipples
mouths open and dumb
eyes blind
in real life orgasm

in the *Saal zur Kaufleuten*, April 1919
they went beserk at the name of Napoleon and he wasn't
    even Swiss
1982 videos of battles in approved areas
shoot silent up old men's veins
a star falls
American satelites
declare no place isolated
every detail ignored

lost rooms escape camera gaze
rural Thai girls in one-way mirror city parlors
are gang-fucked by Japanese business men
a delicate culture
they make Papageno do it with Papagena in feathers
stuttering outside the temple

they breed like flies
in cells without number
TVs spawn Lady Death
a nation's sweetheart
her Prince grows celluloid horns caressed by wood
    - tongued this - England
                               ladies
in Wiltshire and Virginia

not a dry eye in East Finchley or
from four miles out the centre of any US city
Chicago Irish and cockney mothers dream of Snow White
    and the seven dwarfs

what hope for a pear tree on a May morning
a last fuck in the ambulance
before bankers pop-eyed on the shift
'a few tight spots old chap
lost a few ghurkas'
in native languages the function of grammar
and verbal meaning are often confused
in a remarkable manner

it is summer and four tastefully dressed Swedes get out of a
vintage white Bentley which they park by a field which has
wild flowers in it

in Umeå accountants, farmers, salesmen
in lightweight suits under red lamps
dance old-time waltzes of muted adulteries
finishing at midnight in no magic night
in New York City lines round the block
queue in heat to see 900 Picassos
a black derelict whimpers
'buy a pencil for the grace of God.'

earth under terror
gut fear at the heart
a great host crying
tighten my belt I remember Churchill I love you
charity leaves poisoned food on the doorstep

we must carry out death past the vesper fixers
you can catch the sun in a cat's cradle
we laugh
it is a webbed sun
a life of its own
                      as Heisenberg sd
we take the string off our fingers
the sun escapes

there are no equivalents
only gesture and our words
the ensemble of events is given
always something for nothing if you're quick enough
or can sit still

split log ends make fractions in standing waves
they rise in dark intervals
root tap-root fibre stem-growth forest
we stretch ropes singing a world-making song
can you catch a bird's nest in a fog
running by a valley's edge?

no voice from the mountain but what we give back
or we suffer under sentence
as much expect life from a fossil or
eternal beauty
a hand's grasp breaks logic
suffered
        parted towards opened eyes and loosened tongues
the silence of gold is four naked virgins in a temple
with throats uncut
Schoenberg unwrites the writ
Time Magazine holds a match over
cracker-barrel staves

tells me a million and a half people will die in Africa this
     year
of starvation

crops turn to cash
forests to ashes
               US mystery initiators inaugurate the big trust
Reagan chops wood on TV
fraternizing patricians submit the third world to the third
     degree
a darkness visible
amazed in Orient
bound to hele
care lost between cancer and cure

trembling before the machine
our hands join
the stranger is ourselves
she must speak
he must speak
we will not be silent.

song for H.
who said
'what is romanticism?'

---

music begins it

tears of dissonance
discovered in
a ringing of changes

a sweet slow fount
John Jenkyn's music
sounds in that body
which is your heart

a chambered music or
chamber music
lies in this dark room
its recorded wildness of viols
practices us with those errors
we learn in craft
to perform

so that
    the words
    set themselves
    for more brilliant divisions

so that
    pale Northwoman
    your heart beats
in the whole turning of your body

a politics of life treasure
a room's sage
breast breath swelled serpent down wallcliff
flood enfolded   shelter on headland
heart courage of hearth companions

*waegliðendum wide gesyne**

fire in freckled face
voice quiet in sound depths

a thing undergone
so that we are compelled to listen for the notes
for that fragment
               which is a melodic line

your breasts to my touch
flow in a new space of your body's curve
adapting without design
to shape
a twined spiral
of more than the sum of these bodies' parts

a movement across memory a beat measured
to laughter of well-tempered keys

a clavichord's crescendo
sounds in attentive ears
rises
until a music of a distant room begins -
engulfs this heart

* From *Beowulf*, L. 3158 "for wave-farers widely visible".

Linton Kwesi Johnson

Sonny's Lettah
(Anti-Sus poem)

                                          Brixton Prison,
                                          Jebb Avenue,
                                          London SW2,
                                          England

Dear Mama,
Good Day.
I hope dat wen
deze few lines reach y'u,
they may find y'u in di bes' af helt.

Mama,
I really doan know how fi tell y'u dis,
cause I did mek a salim pramis
fi tek care a lickle Jim
an' try mi bes' fi look out fi him.

Mama,
Ah really did try mi bes',
but non-di-les',
mi sarry fi tell y'u seh
poor lickle Jim get arres'.

It woz di miggle a di rush howah
wen everybady jus' a hus'le an' a bus'le
fi goh home fi dem evenin' showah;
mi an' Jim stan-up
waitin' pan a bus,
nat causin' no fus',
wen all an a sudden'
a police van pull-up.

Out jump t'ree policeman,
di 'hole a dem carryin' batan.
Dem waak straight up to mi an' Jim.
One a dem hol' an to Jim
seh him tekin him in;
Jim tell him fi let goh a him
far him noh dhu not'n',
an him naw t'ief,
nat even a but'n.
Jim start to wriggle.
Di police start to giggle.

Mama,
mek Ah tell y'u whey dem dhu to Jim;
Mama,
mek Ah tell y'u whey dem dhu to him:

dem t'ump him in him belly
an' it turn to jelly
dem lick him pan him back
an' him rib get pap
dem lick him pan him he'd
but it tuff like le'd
dem kick him in him seed
an' it started to bleed

Mama,
Ah jus' could'n' stan-up deh
an' noh dhu not'n':

soh mi jook one in him eye
an' him started to cry;
mi t'ump one in him mout'
an' him started to shout

mi kick one pan him shin
an' him started to spin
mi t'ump him pan him chin
an' him drap pan a bin

an' crash
an de'd.

Mama,
more policeman come dung
an' beat mi to di grung;
dem charge Jim fi sus;
dem charge mi fi murdah.

Mama
doan fret,
doan get depres'
an' doun-hearted
Be af good courage
till I hear fram you.

I remain,
your son,
Sonny.

Reggae fi Dada

galang dada
galang gwaan yaw sah
yu nevah ad noh life fi live
jus di wan life fi give
yu did yu time pan ert
yu nevah get yu just dizert
galang goh smile inna di sun
galang goh satta inna di palace af peace

o di waatah
it soh deep
di waatah
it soh daak
an it full a hawbah shaak

di lan is like a rack
slowly shattahrin to san
sinkin in a sea af calimity
where fear breed shadows
dat lurks in di daak
where people fraid fi waak
fraid fi tink fraid fi taak
where di present is haunted by de paas

a deh soh mi bawn
get fi know bout staam
learn fi cling to di dawn
an wen mi hear mi daddy sick
mi quickly pack mi grip an tek a trip

mi nevah have noh time
wen mi reach
fi si noh sunny beach
wen mi reach
jus people a live in shack
people livin back-to-back
mongst cackroach an rat
mongst dirt an dizeez
subjek to terrorist attack
political intrigue
kanstant grief
an noh sign af relief

o di grass
turn brown
soh many trees
cut doun
an di lan is ovahgrown

fram country to town
is jus thistle an tawn
inna di woun a di poor
is a miracle ow dem endure
di pain nite an day
di stench af decay
di glarin sights
di guarded affluence
di arrogant vices
cole eyes af kantemp
de mackin symbals af independence

a deh soh mi bawn
get fi know bout staam
learn fi cling to di dawn

an wen di news reach mi
seh mi wan daddy ded
mi ketch a plane quick

an wen mi reach mi sunny isle
it woz di same ole style
di money well dry
di bullits dem a fly
plenty innocent a die
many rivahs run dry
ganja plane flyin high
di poor man im a try
yu tink a lickle try im try
holdin awn bye an bye
wen a dallah cant buy
a lickle dinnah fi a fly

galang dada
galang gwaan yaw sah
you nevah ad noh life fi live
just di wan life fi give
yu did yu time pan ert
yu nevah get yu jus dizert
galang goh smile inna di sun
galang goh satta inna di palace af peace

mi know yu couldn tek it dada
di anguish an di pain
di suffahrin di prablems di strain
di strugglin in vain
fi mek two ens meet
soh dat dem pickney coulda get
a lickle someting fi eat

fi put cloaz pan dem back
fi put shoes pan dem feet
wen a dallah cant buy
a lickle dinnah fi a fly

mi know yu try dada
yu fite a good fite
but di dice dem did loaded
an di card pack fix
yet still yu reach fifty-six
before yu lose yu leg wicket
'a noh yu bawn grung here'
soh wi bury yu a Stranger's Burying Groun
near to mhum an cousin Daris
nat far fram di quarry
doun a August Town

Life

Farness, of an evening, tends to disturb me.
Migratory birds, when they pass in the dusk,
appear to travel so certainly southwards,
that it makes me fidget about in my hutch
with its double-glazing. But, although dulling
my life with dreams of sunshine, I know grasping
my fortune is not my style. I never leave.
My gaze never quits the table till told.

Why then, when I ridicule girls whose fear of
flying makes them angry enough to lift off,
do I take out the car to listen to one
who reads his poems about escaping? Think
(is their gist) of marriages and begettings
as throwaway pedal- bin liners whose start
is crisp, but who soon become messy, always
about to rupture until, finally, dumped!

Is this affable entertainer really
the man who survived three nuclear families,
who hit road upon road to find freedom blooms best
in travail among ruined relationships?
I give him his book to sign and be spatters
his letters across the page like sperm. To you
(I read) affectionately! Little wonder
birds jostle to nest with that golden gossoon!

At coffee one such wants to hear his credo.
Omphalopsychic urges (he replies)
are forms of the death-wish. I flee the still hub.

I dance along the peripheries. As Freud
means joy, lady, you must fuck it or funk it!
Each morning I and my Puer kiss. We then
rape Mother. And Senex, his husbandhood lost,
- now how do you British say? - soon pops his clogs.

Jesus, how the stark transatlantic sickens!
I drive back to husband-fixations, and back
to nearness, sweet daughter of morning. Breakfast
consoles me. Cornflakes (I read) are sunshine. Birds
flutter around the package. Smiling tigers
promise to lick. To you, affectionately,
crackles and snaps! And I tell the table
that 'near is the living god and hard to grasp.'

The Wards in Jarndyce

When Richard dies, his face on Ada's boson,
'...and with one parting sob begins the world',
we cry. Not that we show it much. With forty,
no rebels now against environment
or schooling, we're a couple who have seen
love close to lovelessness, yet remained dry-eye'd.

At seventeen, how otherwise! Tchaikovsky
exacted sobs and sex. Sinatra, too!
We hiccupped ecstasy into the refuge
of musty cushions, pooled our fluids in
defiance of conspiracies downstairs.
Yes, all the night made we our beds to swim!

Such gut - upheavals seemed tasteless within
a family expanding. So we said
at thirty-three: Enough! This shaping up
for crucifixion is pretentious. We are here
to blubber in the background when Christ dies,
our faces signs that show: guilt is collective.

Fifty-ish. more shrugging off. And living down.
Tears tucked like secrets into nighttime whispers.
All tell-tale stains laundered by breakfast-time!
And, children, you can trust us, too, with paper
and TV. Scenes of life lambasting life,
the martyr's groan, the lover's sigh: no comment!

Then three-score years and ten. And we'll be facing
our children's children, tired now of tight lips.
Life's ironies will out! We'll hear them quote:
'I have had a good cry...obliged to lock
myself in...my face was swollen to twice
its proper size...hugely ridiculous!'

They'll diagnose: 'You're locked up in yourselves!
It's not that important!'...Nonsense! We'll show
them how, in dying, one can outface all!
...or, should we cast masks to the ending world
and, laughing, sobbing, swollen-faced, unbosom
our tale: one nest, two chicks, a sudden parting?

Folly

These many years a beanstalk, I, and you,
a little titch, have wheeled this birthday-bike.

An adam-appled show-off capers to your
allure: look! Cable brakes, Sturmey-Archer
three-speed, pink tubular tomfoolery...

That makes you laugh. You say: let's walk. A mile
or so I push my bike, you holding on
off-side. The front tyre lifts its clean, black tread
like the paw of a listening gazelle.
The firm frame between us trembles, knowing.

Paired in shyness under a brilliant sky.
But time! What time there is comes fast, too fast!
Just past my britching-time, what gentleness
I know of I lavish on the handle-bars;
my fingers stroke reflections in the chrome.

They fondle the soft leather of a badge,
proficiency's award. Then, whilst I vaunt
my finesse in straight steering, you let go.
The moment punctures beyond repairing.
Silence, a third party, mounts the saddle.

That cursed bike took how many birthdays
to rattle towards desuetude? When, at last
I dumped it, I split its spokes with kicks, cheered
my stubbed toe! - But memory laughs. Boot-proof
it whispers at night: let's walk. Once again

I pick up my pink-and-silver folly
and wonder, after a mile or so skirting
insomnia, why the sun should sit so blackly
in a dull sky, why the road which nearly led
to you and me, still travels the other way?

Madness

And if the wind gets in before the train does?
Anxiety finds waiting-room in closets
beneath the station stairs. I dither watching
the river rise, knowing full well insomniacs,
fearful of noises jangling before noon-time,
have set the flood-alerts. I ask if going
is our sole option. People say: be quiet!
and if the wind gets in before the train does?

My habitat has always been a flatness.
In sleep, sometimes, my toes curl round nightmarish
unevennesses, but diagnosticians
have never mentioned more than pills or diets.
So, all in all, nothing to send one packing!
I tell my dogs, mates, offspring: let us worry
when newscasts start to focus on real bulges.
My habitat has always been a flatness.

Departure in my scheme of things needs platforms
from which leave-taking can be studied. How to
go in for tears, heart-rending? Such emotions
will want adapting to. I know that Nietzsche
said: travel or you die! But who to read, if,
accustomed to stand back and sadly waving,
yet comfortably, one sticks to the same station?
Departure in my scheme of things needs platforms.

Fire will erase, that is what last night's film showed,
a race of men who spend their lives positioning
their garden gnomes. Madness will burst from squabbles
over herbaceous borders squelched by children.

Then dying will be monitored in shelters
by leaders, petulant, the film suggested,
at having nothing to berate but ashes.
Fire will erase! That is what last night's film showed.

Lizzie's well

Old Lizzie Stapleton, who died a while back,
was gathering mushrooms on the flank of the hill.
The morning was damp. A patch of mist still clung
to the thorn-tree, the one crouched with its gnarled roots
over the flag-stoned well-mouth. Lizzie, always
sure good water, and also Fynnon Salts, would
rid her of back-ache, knelt down for a mouthful.

Plain murder, the bending down! But through her pain
she noticed a sudden ceasing of bird-song.
When, oh, with a brightness of brightness gleaming,
veils of blueness eddied over the thorn-tree.
Lizzie, crossing herself, could see the Virgin,
the Blessed Virgin, yes, coming at her through
the ripples. then vanish. She was smiling, but
sadly, Lizzie maintained, fit to pierce your heart!

After milking we like passing the time of day
with the motorised offspring of Lizzie's farm;
youngsters on the dole, some working in Woolworth's.
Ireland's song in the Eurovision contest,
a close thing, that! Teach England a trick or two!

We glance up the tree-less hill-side, a dome of
dusk chequered with still glowing splurges of wheat;
and fog like a veil over the spot where down
cemented gullies the hill's spring-water drains off.

A Tale of Hoffmann

The house draws back like a startled watch-dog.
Which of the windows will open and bark?
I watch you mounting the steps. Oh, dear one,
why did you curtsy with an empty smile?

You drolleries, were they my dismissal?
Now the red front-door has started to snarl!
Please, watch out! It is trained to be savage.
Its fangs will surely rip you to pieces.

I don't understand what is happening!
The house lies crouched at your feet. You pat it,
walk on into drooling shadows. Of course:
you are the owner's wife. You have the leash.

In the garden, where the trees are, a tail
is wagging. Your voice coos: doggie loves me!
It bites my life in two. The house howls and
flings itself at me. I kick it and run.

Pauline Melville

Mixed

Sometimes, I think
My mother with her blue eyes
And flowered apron
Was exasperated
At having such a sallow child,
And my mulatto daddee
Silenced
By having such an English-looking one.

And so my mother
Rubbed a little rouge on my cheeks
For school,
Lest people should think
She was not doing her job properly.

And my father chose to stay at home
On sports days.

Hideous Love

I was never reasonable.
I am the woman in the Chalk Circle
Who would not let go,
Rage and chicken feathers
My north star.

Perhaps I should not
Have made my home in your dreams,

You, of all people,
The arch-wolf in a pewter sea.
But I did - like a soucriant.
And when you left
I ran, knife in hand
Through the skies of Paris -
That city of romance and Alsation dogs.
Some people even reported a ball of fire
Over Notre Dame.
Later, I took to wandering
Through the markets of foreign cities
Calling your name.

My love dwindled into a hyena
Nosing with blood-stained snout
Over carcasses of memory.

They say time is a great healer,
So I wait for events
To clamp their sutures
Round the wound.

Meanwhile, the wind howls
Through empty sheets.
My house is a tomb
That I inhabit
On the level of poetry and cutlasses,
Dressed all in white,
Like a seagull.

Homeland

The old colonial house,
My father's birthplace,
White shuttered, wooden slatted,
Sags and settles on its haunches.
A lewd stripteaze of peeling paint
Reveals grey, sun-bleached timbers,
Exposing the house for what it is -
A brothel.

Relentlessly indifferent,
The sun hangs, a metallic sphere in space,
Over the small town of New Amsterdam.

History too, it seems,
Tired of the sandflies,
Has packed its bags and emigrated
From this land of many waters
Somewhere behind God's back.

I am standing
On the dark, varnished wooden floor,
Mosquito nets - obscene bridal veils
Hang in the breezeless air.
My father, as a child,
Leans from the window,
Gazing out,
Eyes deep with unfathomable histories,
At the armies of clouds that march
Across the wide, wide skies from Venezuela,
Destined for other horizons.
Eventually, he was to follow them.

Darkness falls.
Together we listen to the tree-frogs
Outside the house
Which perches so precariously
On the edge of this vast continent
Of perpetual decay.
And a voice wails out
From the ancient juke-box in the bottom-house:
'Take me by the hand
And lead me to the land
Of ecstasy.'

For Abbyssinian and Andaiye

Cove and John

The black woman
With the beautiful scar on her lip
Cultivated a library in the forest.
Histories of the lives of Amerindians
Blossomed under the tatabu tree;
Volumes of Lenin multiplied in the fertile earth;
Novels from Europe flourished
Among the jacaranda and the dragon-tongue shrubs.
Quietly and with determination
She nurtured the library.

The woman's brother,
Fair-skinned, blue-eyed,
Dreadlocks like twisted ropes of liana,
Grew pictures in the forest.
Butterflies flew into his paintings;
Miraculously tiny flowers sang there.

Together with their friends
They created a sanctuary
At Cove and John
For all these things to be preserved
Till freedom time.

Meanwhile, the mad negro
Who dressed in purple
Mimicking emperors,
Regularly rode his white horse nearby.
One day he commanded his forces
To raid the library in the forest.

But poetry was a code they could not crack.
The paintings they held this way and that
And could not decipher.
As they left, puzzled,
The hibiscus blooms all turned
And put out their tongues.

The enraged horseman
With the terrible voice
Bellowed at the raggedy-pants children of many races:
'Where are your fathers?
They should be working in my house
And on my land.'

But the children just giggled and sang:
'Daddy gone. Daddy gone.
Daddy gone to Cove and John.'

Stonebridge Park Estate

Hyacinth is not yet used
To living in the sky.
She sits, jangling gold bangles,
Chains and anklets,
On the magic red patterned carpet,
T.V. in the corner,
Eating figs.

A cold wind howls through
The derelict haunted walkways in space.
The lift with steel doors
Hums upwards towards the North Star.

Hyacinth sits in state
In her small room in the sky,
Hair braided and beaded,
Elbow on the carved leather footstool from home,
Hand upon her jaw,
Watching 'Dynasty'.

A piece of El Dorado in Harlesden.

Mandela

Rain, rain, rain, listen to the rain drum
On the plains of Afrika
Hear the rain drum.

On the tin shack roofs of Soweto
Hear the rain drum
Drumming out the name

Mandela Mandela Mandela Mandela Mandela Mandela
    Mandela
Business men try to pull down the shutters
But the rain come drumming on the window pane

Mandela Mandela Mandela Mandela Mandela Mandela
    Mandela
Deep in the forest
Hear the parakeet screech the name Biko Biko Biko

In Afrika there is a gathering storm
And the hooves of the herds as they wheel on the plain
Are thundering the name

MANDELA MANDELA MANDELA MANDELA
    MANDELA MANDELA MANDELA
For the roar of the lion
Brings skyscrapers down
Raises up the shanty town
And the name of the lion -

MANDELA

The Poets

Alison Brackenbury was born in Britain and is presently based in Cheltenham. She is widely recognised as one of the leading poets in Britain today and has published widely in a variety of literary magazines (*Poetry Review, PN Review, Literary Review* etc.). Her first collection, *Dreams of Power* 1981, was a Poetry Book Society recommendation. Her second collection, *Breaking Ground,* was published by Carcanet Press in 1984. A third collection is due to be published in 1988.

Clive Bush was born in Britain in 1942. After doing his voluntary service in Nigeria in 1960/1, he entered King's College, London to read English. He currently teaches American Literature at the University of Warwick. He has published two collections of poetry and a major study of American culture, *The Dream of Reason: American consciousness and cultural achievement 1776-1865* (1978).

David Dabydeen was born in Guyana and came to England in 1969. He went to secondary school in south London then to the University of Cambridge where he read English. After a post- doctoral Junior Research Fellowship at the University of Oxford, and a brief period at Yale University, he moved to the University of Warwick to take up a Lectureship, in 1984. His first book of poems, *Slave Song* was awarded the Commonwealth Poetry Prize and Cambridge University Quiller-Couch Prize. His second collection is entitled *Coolie Odyssey* (1988).

Linton Kwesi Johnson was born in Clarendon, Jamaica in 1952. He has lived in Britain since 1963. He was educated at Tulse Hill Secondary Comprehensive School, London, and Goldsmiths' College, University of London (BA Hons. Sociology). In 1977 he was Writer-in-Residence in the London Borough of Lambeth. Since graduating from University he has worked as a free-lance journalist, broadcaster and recording artist. His three collections of poems are *Voices of the Living and the Dead* (Race Today Publications, 1974), *Dread Beat an' Blood* (Bogle-L'Ouverture, 1975) and *Inglan is a Bitch*

(Race Today, 1980). His albums are: 'Dread Beat an' Blood' (Virgin Records, 1978), 'Forces of Victory' (Island Records, 1979), 'Bass Culture' (Island Records, 1980), 'LKJ in Dub' (Island Records, 1981), 'Making History' (Island Records, 1984), 'Reggae Greats' (Island Records, 1985) and 'LKJ in Concert' (LKJ/Rough Trade, 1985). Johnson is the arts editor of the journal *Race Today* and a member of the Alliance of the Black Parents Movement and the Race Today Collective.

Rolf Lass was born in Belgium in 1936 of English/German parentage. He went to school in Britain, Ireland and Germany, and studied at the University of Cambridge for his doctorate. He has been teaching English and Comparative Literature at Warwick since 1966, and spent 1987/8 as a Visiting Lecturer at the University of the West Indies (Cave Hill Campus, Barbados).

Pauline Melville was born in England to an English mother and a Guyanese father. Her work in England has been mainly in the theatre, as an actress. She has also appeared in several films and television series. In Jamaica she has worked with the Sistren Theatre Collective and done some teaching at the Jamaican School of Drama. She also worked briefly in Grenada during the Maurice Bishop régime, taking theatre workshops. She is presently working on a postgraduate thesis at the University of Warwick. This is the first time she has published her poetry.